P9-BHZ-395

Level C

Reading Explorations

Globe Fearon

Writers: Joanne Suter and Sandra Widener
Senior Editor: Nance Davidson
Project Editors: Marion Castellucci, Amy Jolin,
          Robert McIlwaine
Production Editor: Rosann Bar
Electronic Page Production: Heather Roake
Electronic Art: Armando Baez

Printed in the United States of America
  3 4 5 6 7 8 9 10   01 00 99 98

ISBN 0-835-93440-3

Globe Fearon Educational Publisher
A Division of Simon & Schuster
Upper Saddle River, New Jersey

Contents

Social Studies

History shows how the past is important. In this section, you'll read about interesting people and ideas that haven't been forgotten.

Early Olympic Games

WORDS TO KNOW

chariot race (CHAR-ee-uht rays) a race of carts with two wheels pulled by horses

pentathlon (pehn-TATH-lahn) a sports contest that tests skills in five events

discus (DIHS-kuhs) a heavy plate of metal or wood. Throwing it is a test of strength.

javelin (JAV-lihn) a light spear

armor (AHR-muhr) a suit of metal worn to protect the body against weapons

Long ago, the people of Greece held contests to honor a god. They tested skills in sports. Athletes were proud to be examples from their cities. They were happy to show their abilities in the first Olympic Games.

Every four years, athletes from around the world meet. They try to show they are best in their sport. Crowds cheer in the stands. All over the world, people watch on TV. The spirit of the Olympics excites us all.

That spirit began almost 3,000 years ago. Let's go back in time to when the Olympics began.

It was late summer in Greece, a small country in Europe. The sun was hot. Fields were ripe with grapes and olives. A parade marched down the dusty roads. The five days of the Olympic Games were about to begin.

1. How long ago were the first Olympic Games?

2. Where did the Olympics begin?

Men in purple robes led the parade. They were the judges. The athletes followed. They came from all the lands nearby.

There were no games on the first day of the Olympics. The athletes stood before a statue of their most important god. They raised their hands. They swore to follow all the rules of the games. The judges, too, raised their hands. They swore they would be fair.

There was peace that day in the country. The cities of Greece had been at war. But all battles stopped during the games. The athletes were as proud of winning contests as they were of winning battles.

The second day of the Olympics started with the sound of horns. The **chariot race** was first. Drivers shouted to their horses. Bright carts bounced around the track. Some tipped over.

A red chariot won the race! The owner stepped up. He heard his name, the name of his father, and the name of his city. He got a crown of olive leaves. The driver got a band of wool.

The best part of the third day was the **pentathlon**. It had five parts. The athletes threw a **discus** and a **javelin**. They did a long jump. They ran a foot race. They wrestled.

The athlete that won the most contests was the winner of the pentathlon.

On the fourth day there were three contests. There was a foot race. This was a short run of 600 feet. A win in this race was the highest honor in the games.

Boxing was next. These violent matches had no rest times. There were no rules against hitting a man when he was down. The boxers fought until one was knocked out.

Last was a very hard race. The runners were soldiers. They wore **armor** to protect them in wars. In the early Olympics, these soldiers ran 1,200 feet dressed in their heavy metal suits.

There were no games on the fifth day. The winners stood before the statue of their god. They wore crowns of olive leaves. They believed that the circle of leaves linked them to the gods.

The athletes enjoyed a feast. The Olympic Games came to a close. The crowds started their long trip home. The Olympic peace soon ended. The cities of Greece went back to war.

The Greeks held Olympic Games for 1,200 years. Then the games ended.

Many years passed. In 1896, the first modern Olympics were held. Today, the olive crowns are gone. Athletes get medals instead. Many of the games are new. But the Olympic spirit is the same. Athletes still come together in peace. They meet for the world's greatest tests of skill.

3. Why did battles stop during the early Olympics?

4. What do you think made the pentathlon a hard event?

5. How were winning athletes honored?

6. What is the same about the early Olympics and today's Olympics? What is different?

7. In what way do you think the Olympic Games are important to our world?

Salem Witch Hunts

WORDS TO KNOW

witches (WIHCH-ihz) people believed to have magical powers to hurt others

preacher (PREE-chuhr) a person who gives talks about God, usually at a church

Tituba (TIH-tyoo-buh) an African American woman in the story

bewitched (bih-WIHCHD) to be under a witch's power

trial (treyel) a place where a person's guilt or innocence is decided

Long ago, people asked, "Why do bad things happen?" Some blamed gods or bad spirits. In 1692, some people blamed **witches.**

In 1692, a lot of people believed in witches. They thought some people had special power to hurt others. Today, that is hard to understand. However, at that time, people were afraid.

Salem was a very small town in Massachusetts. The whole village was just some farms, a meeting house, and a tavern.

In 1692, Salem got a new **preacher** for its church. Samuel Parris came to the village. He was not happy. He wanted to lead a church in a large town. Instead, he got Salem. Salem was too small for him.

Parris came with his wife. They brought their two daughters. They also brought two African Americans, **Tituba** and John.

Parris was a hard man. In church, he put fear into people. He raised his arms and roared. He wanted people to be good. They saw the preacher's angry eyes. They were afraid to be bad.

Tituba came from the South. Her home was an island. It was a land of sun and songs. Winter in Salem was cold and dull for her.

Tituba worked in the kitchen, close to the fire. The two Parris daughters, Abigail and Betsey, spent their days with her.

To pass the time, Tituba told the girls stories. They were the tales she had learned as a child. She spoke of "Duppy," a man who could talk to the dead. She spoke about magic. Some of her stories were scary.

Soon, the kitchen was full of young women. The tales scared them. But they always came back for more.

1. What was Parris's job?

2. Why did Parris dislike Salem?

3. Where was Tituba from?

The kitchen meetings went on all winter. Then one cold night a young woman in Salem woke up with a scream. She sat up in her bed. She yelled. Her eyes rolled back in her head. She was having a fit. "A witch is after me!" she cried. It seemed that Anne Putnam had heard too many scary tales.

The doctor came. He looked at Anne. "The girl is **bewitched**. She must be under the magical power of a witch," he said.

Soon Anne was the talk of the village. Then, young Mercy Lewis had a fit, too. Not long after that, Abigail Parris screamed in the night.

"There must be a witch in Salem!" people said. "Name her," they told the young women. The witch hunt began.

They pointed to a ragged beggar. "Sarah Good is a witch!" they said. They named Sarah Osborne, too. She was a sick old woman whom few people liked. Then they named Tituba.

The young women found they had great power. They could name anyone they wanted. Those people would be put in jail.

All three women went to jail. Each had a **trial**. The judges of the court said they were witches. The women had to agree or they would die.

Sarah Good would not say she was a witch. She was hanged. Sarah Osborne died in jail. Tituba saw no choice. She said she was a witch. She was not killed.

Those were the first witch trials. During the next year, the jail filled with those named as witches. Most were women. A few were men. Nineteen people were hanged.

At last people came to their senses. They knew awful mistakes had been made. The witch hunts ended in May 1693. Those still in jail were set free.

4. What do you think caused Anne Putnam to have a fit?

5. What did the doctor say about what was wrong with Anne?

6. Why do you think the young women chose certain people to name as witches?

7. Why wasn't Tituba killed?

8. Do you think the young women would be so easily believed today? Why? Why not?

The Muckrakers

WORDS TO KNOW

---

muckrakers (MUK-rayk-uhrz) newspaper writers during the early 1900s

Ida Tarbell (EYE-duh TAHR-behl) a muckraker who wrote about business

Jacob Riis (JAY-kuhb rees) a muckraker who wrote about poor people

slums (slumz) crowded, run-down places where poor people live

Upton Sinclair (UP-tuhn sihn-KLAIR) a muckraker who wrote about meat packing

---

Muckrakers were writers who called for action against things that were wrong. They wanted to make life better in the United States in the early 1900s.

The word *muck* means "dirt." A muckraker is one who "rakes up the muck." He or she "digs up the dirt" by finding out what is wrong or unfair.

The muckrakers of the early 1900s dug deep to find what was wrong. Then they picked up their pens. They told others what they knew. They tried to make things right.

1. What is a muckraker?

2. How did muckrakers get their name?

In 1900, big business was booming. Lots of people got rich. But many people were also poor. The muckrakers wrote about the poor. They also wrote about the rich.

Ida Tarbell was a muckraker. She dug up the dirt on big business. Her father had run a small oil company. Standard Oil was a huge company. It easily put Ida Tarbell's father out of business.

Tarbell learned all about Standard Oil. In 1902, she wrote a book about it. Her book was called *History of the Standard Oil Company*.

It told of unfair deals. It told how the giants of big business killed small businesses. The book made people mad. They passed laws to control big business.

Jacob Riis was a New York newsman. He knew the city's poor. He saw where they lived. He thought the **slums** were terrible.

Riis wrote *How the Other Half Lives*. His book looked at life in a slum. "Everyone on the floor uses one sink. In summer, the smells from the sinks poison everyone."

Riis told about rats. He told about the smell of old trash. He made people see life in the slums. His work led to help for the poor.

The writer **Upton Sinclair** did his muckraking in Chicago. He went to the meat plants. He saw cows killed. He saw meat packed.

Sinclair saw meat on the floor. He saw it scooped up with bits of dead rats and wood. This mess was made into hot dogs. It also went into canned ham.

"It was enough to make anybody sick, to think people had to eat such stuff as this," Sinclair wrote in *The Jungle*. The book was about the meat packing plants. It came out in 1906. Soon, new laws were passed to keep food clean and safe.

Tarbell, Riis, and Sinclair were just three muckrakers. There were more. They could have had quiet lives as writers. But they made sure they were heard. They wanted to help people. They dug up the truth. Then they held it up for all to see.

3. What happened because of Tarbell's book about Standard Oil?

4. How did Riis get people to care about the poor?

5. Why was Sinclair upset about meat packing plants?

6. Why do you think these people became muckrakers?

7. Why were muckrakers important in the early 1900s?

Jim Thorpe

If you gave Jim Thorpe a ball, he would throw it the farthest. If you put him in a race, he would run the fastest. Jim Thorpe may have been the greatest athlete ever.

The story of Jim Thorpe is one of talent, spirit, and fame. It is also one of heartbreak and sadness.

Jim Thorpe and his twin brother Charlie were born in 1888. Their family was Native American. Thorpe's great-grandfather was Chief Black Hawk. He was the leader of the Sac and Fox group.

The twins were close as they grew up. They played on their ranch in **Oklahoma**. Both boys loved sports.

When they were six, the boys went away to the Sac and Fox school. It was 23 miles from home. Right away, the twins stood out. Jim came in first in every sport. Charlie came in close behind him.

One day Charlie Thorpe got sick. There were no doctors to help him. Charlie died.

Jim Thorpe was shocked by his brother's death. He was very unhappy. Even the games were no fun now. He ran away from school.

Thorpe's parents sent him to a second school. It was even farther from the ranch. Now Thorpe would not be able to run home.

At the new school, Thorpe played football. The older players were wide-eyed when they saw him play.

Then, Thorpe heard his father was hurt. He took off. It took him two weeks to get home. When he got there, his father was better. Soon after, though, his mother got sick and died suddenly.

1. Where did Jim Thorpe grow up?

2. What happened to his brother?

3. What happened to his mother?

When Thorpe was 15, he went to a third boarding school. Bad news greeted him. He learned that his father had died. He also learned that he was too young and too small to play football.

Jim Thorpe was all alone now. He was strong, though. He wanted to make it. He knew he could work hard. He wasn't sure he could do it by himself. Maybe someone would help him.

Thorpe was right. Soon, one of the school's coaches spotted him. Everyone called Coach Glenn Warner "Pop." Pop Warner saw Thorpe play football. "That boy is something!" he said.

Pop started Thorpe on the track team. "You're still too small for football," he told Jim. "But you can run!"

Thorpe also played baseball. He played basketball and tennis. He even went out for the swimming team. At each sport, he was the best.

In 1907, Pop Warner gave Thorpe a football uniform. Thorpe was strong. He ran fast. No one could stop the new player.

One summer, Thorpe was out of school and alone. He needed money. He took a job. He played baseball for $15 a week. That summer job would haunt Thorpe years later.

Thorpe went back to school in the fall. He played ball for Pop. He never said a word about his summer job.

"The time has come," Pop said to Thorpe one day. "I think you have what it takes to make the Olympic team."

The Olympics is a contest of the world's best athletes. It is held every four years. In Thorpe's time, all athletes were supposed to be **amateurs**. They were supposed to play sports just for fun. They were not allowed to play for money.

Thorpe did not know he had to be an amateur. He did not say anything about the baseball job. He made the 1912 U.S. Olympic team without any trouble. He went to Sweden for the games. Sweden is a country in the northern part of Europe.

Thorpe could play just about any sport. He was perfect for the **decathlon**. This contest had 10 events.

Thorpe won the gold medal. He scored 700 points higher than the man who came in second. That was an athlete from Sweden. Thorpe also won the five events of the pentathlon.

America cheered Jim Thorpe. They welcomed home their hero, the great-grandson of a Sac and Fox chief.

Then things changed. Word got out. Jim Thorpe had been paid to play baseball. It did not matter that he only made $15 a week. It did not matter that it was a summer job. That job meant he was not an amateur. It meant he should not have been on the Olympic team.

Thorpe knew he was not the only one. Other Olympic athletes had played ball to earn money. Some had not used their own names. Thorpe had been honest. He lost his Olympic title. He had to give back his medals.

The second place Swedish athlete would not take the medal. "It is not mine!" he said. "The greatest athlete in the world is Jim Thorpe!"

Native Americans felt Thorpe's pain. Some thought he'd been wronged by white America.

But Jim Thorpe was not finished with sports. He played **professional** baseball. He played **pro** football. He made his living at sports until 1930. In 1953, Thorpe died of a heart attack.

Much later, in 1982, the Olympics had a change of heart. They decided they had been unfair. They put Thorpe's name back on the list of winners. But it was too late for Thorpe. He never knew he got his medals back.

4. Why did Thorpe take a summer job playing baseball?

5. What was the Olympic rule about amateurs?

6. Why was Thorpe just right for the decathlon?

7. Why did Thorpe lose his Olympic medals?

8. Do you think it was right that Thorpe had to give back the medals? Why? Why not?

9. Who do you think is the greatest athlete in the world today?

Science

Science opens a new world.
Learn about seasons, sunlight,
and lasers. Then read about
one scientist who tried to
protect our world.

The Changing Seasons

WORDS TO KNOW

myths (mihths) old stories that try to explain how things happen or came to be

orbit (AWR-biht) the path of one heavenly body going around another

ellipse (ih-LIPS) a closed circle that is shaped like an egg

equator (ee-KWAY-tuhr) an imaginary circle around the middle of Earth. It divides Earth into northern and southern parts.

We shovel snow. We plant flowers and mow the lawn. We rake the leaves. Many of the things we do during the year are tied to the seasons. Read on to find out why the seasons change.

Long ago people were surprised when the seasons changed. They didn't understand what made the leaves fall off the trees. They didn't understand why it got hot. They wanted to be able to explain these changes in nature. They made up **myths** to help themselves understand what was happening.

In Greece, for example, people made up a story to explain winter. They said it came every year when a beautiful young girl had to spend three months in the land of the dead. Then it was winter. When she returned to her mother, spring also returned.

This is an interesting myth. But it really doesn't explain why the seasons change. Today, we know that Earth's tilt causes the seasons. The way Earth circles the sun is another cause.

There are four seasons because of the way Earth moves. It moves in a circle around the sun. This circle is called an **orbit**.

Earth's orbit is not really a perfect circle. The orbit is a flat circle shaped like an egg. That shape is called an **ellipse**.

It takes 365 days for Earth to make one orbit. That is why there are 365 days in a year.

Earth is heated unevenly as it makes its trip around the sun. A few parts of Earth are always warm. People in Hawaii do not really notice the seasons changing because it is warm most of the time. Some other places are almost always cold. Greenland has a very long winter and a very short summer. Greenland is farther north than most other places.

1. Why did people long ago need a story to explain the change of seasons?

2. How long does it take Earth to move all the way around the sun?

Most parts of the world have four seasons. They have hot summers and cold winters. They have rainy springs and cool falls.

There is a reason for the uneven heating of Earth. Earth leans or tilts as it orbits the sun. Earth's tilt does not change. This means that the part of Earth that leans toward the sun is always hotter. The part that leans away from the sun is always colder.

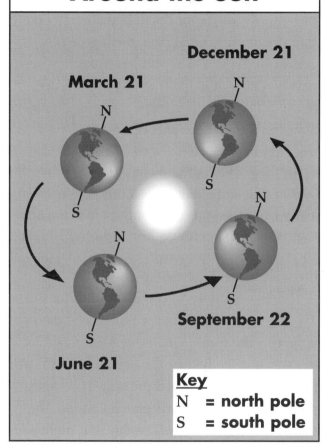

Earth's Orbit Around the Sun

December 21

March 21

N
S

N
S

June 21

September 22

N
S

N
S

Key
N = north pole
S = south pole

Look at the drawing on page 27. It shows Earth at four different times of year. Each time, it is in a different spot in its orbit around the sun. At the top of Earth is the north pole. Each year, on June 21, the north pole tilts closest to the sun. The sun heats the northern part of Earth. It is the first day of summer there. It is warm. There are also more hours of light in the northern part of Earth on June 21 than at any other time of the year. The days seem long. The nights seem short.

On that same date, the south pole is tilted away from the sun. The south pole is the spot that is farthest south on Earth. June 21 is the shortest day of the year in the southern part of the world. It is the first day of winter.

Earth continues to travel around the sun. The days get shorter in the north. The days get longer in the south. On about September 23, the sun is directly over the **equator**. The north pole does not tilt toward the sun. The south pole does not tilt toward the sun either. The sun heats Earth evenly. The day and night are equal everywhere on Earth. There are 12 hours of day and 12 hours of night. This is the first day of fall in the northern part of the world. It is the first day of spring in the south.

On December 21, the north pole tilts farthest away from the sun. The northern part of Earth gets less of the sun's heat. It is the start of winter there.

From this day on, the days become longer in the northern part of the world. They become shorter in the southern part. On March 21, the sun is again directly over the equator. Day and night will be equal everywhere. It is the first day of spring in the northern part of the world. It is the first day of fall in the southern part.

Finally, June 21 rolls around again. Earth has completed its trip around the sun. A year has gone by. It is the first day of summer again in the north. It is the first day of winter again in the south.

3. Describe the shape of the Earth's orbit.

4. If the north pole is tilting away from the sun, what season is it in the northern part of the world?

5. What happens to the hours of light when the south pole tilts toward the sun?

6. If it is summer in the northern part of the world, what season is it in the southern part?

7. When is the sun directly over the equator? What effect does this have on day and night?

8. What are some ways your life changes during the different seasons?

Sunlight

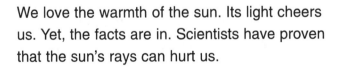

WORDS TO KNOW

scientists (SEYE-uhn-tihstz) people who study, watch, and experiment to learn facts about nature

exposure (ihk-SPOH-zhuhr) the state of being unprotected out in the open

cancer (KAN-suhr) a disease in which some cells grow too fast and kill normal cells

ozone (OH-zohn) one of the gases in the air

We love the warmth of the sun. Its light cheers us. Yet, the facts are in. Scientists have proven that the sun's rays can hurt us.

Sunlight feels good. Its warmth lifts our spirits. But we must take care. The rays of the sun can harm our skin. People with light skin are at greater risk. But the sun can hurt dark skin, too.

People used to think that sitting in the sun was healthy. In the 1980s, we learned the sun was not so healthy after all. **Scientists** studied what the sun does to skin. They found that too much time in the sun is not safe. They said that **exposure** to the sun's rays brings wrinkles. It makes skin look old. Worse than that, scientists said the sun's rays add to the risk of skin **cancer**. This sickness can kill. Many skin doctors had been saying this for years. Now it was certain.

1. Why do people like to sit in the sun?

2. Name two things that can happen to skin that gets too much sun.

The sun's rays have always been bad for skin. But the danger is greater now. People get skin cancer at younger ages. Even teenagers get it. Many sun-lovers find they have wrinkles at the age of 30. Today, more of the sun's rays are finding their way to Earth.

High up in the air, there is a layer of gas called **ozone**. It is known as the ozone layer. Ozone traps harmful rays from the sun. These harmful rays do not reach us on Earth. The ozone layer protects us from them.

The ozone layer is quite thin. Over the years, it stayed pretty much the same. Then we began using chemicals that destroy ozone. We use them in air conditioning, aerosol sprays, and plastics. They float up in the air. They reach the ozone. They break it down. Now, many of the sun's rays do not get trapped. They reach us on Earth. They hurt our skin.

In the 1980s, scientists found that there was less ozone than there had been. They even found a hole in the ozone layer. They warned us to stop using chemicals that break down ozone. The truth became clear. The risks of being in the sun today really are greater than in the past.

Still, we can't stay inside all the time. We must go out into the sun. There are a few ways to protect skin from the sun.

Sunscreens are a great way to guard the skin. Some products protect more than others. Some special sunscreens are even waterproof. Read labels carefully. Rub sunscreen on bare skin before you go out. Put more on every few hours.

A wide-brimmed hat can protect, too. So can clothing. Cover up in the sun. Make sure your clothes don't let the rays through. Thin, white T–shirts let the sun through when they're wet. Wear something else in the sun.

You should be careful about how much sun you get. Too many hours in the sun is not good. Stay out of the sun at midday when it is the strongest.

You should know your own skin. Check it for new growths or changes in old growths. These may be signs of skin cancer. If you find any, tell your doctor. Skin cancer can be cured if it's caught early!

You can still enjoy the warm glow of the sun. But you must be smart. You must be safe in the sun.

3. How does the ozone layer protect us?

4. How can people help the ozone layer?

5. What might happen if more ozone is destroyed?

6. Name two things that protect skin from the sun.

7. Why should you check your skin? What should you look for?

8. Why do people still go out in the sun even when they know it is harmful?

Rachel Carson

WORDS TO KNOW

pests (pehstz) bugs or other creatures that destroy or cause trouble

pesticides (PEHS-tih-seyedz) sprays or powders used to kill bugs

"The birds . . . where had they gone? . . . It was a spring without voices." These are the words of Rachel Carson. They are from her book *Silent Spring*. In it, she warns that we might be destroying our world.

As a child, Rachel Carson won prizes for her stories. She loved to write. She also wanted to be a scientist. She loved to study living things. When she grew up, Carson found a way to write and study science. She wrote books about nature.

In the 1950s, Carson began worrying about nature. People were cutting trees. They were clearing places for homes. Some animals had no place to live. They were dying out. Carson thought we should take better care of wild plants and animals.

Carson picked up her pen. She wrote about wild animals. "Wild creatures, like man, must have a place to live," she wrote.

1. How did Carson mix her love of writing and science?

2. What did she think about wild plants and animals?

Carson worried about what people were doing to nature on farms. It was 1958.

Farmers were at war with bugs. They fought the **pests** that ate crops. They killed these bugs with sprays. They sprayed crops with **pesticides.**

The sprays killed the harmful bugs. But they killed good bugs, too. They killed bees that helped plants bloom. They killed ladybugs and spiders. These good bugs ate bad bugs. Now the good bugs were dead, too.

Some pesticides harmed more than bugs. One was DDT. DDT was sprayed on crops. Rain carried it into rivers and lakes. There it killed fish. Then it killed birds that ate fish. It even harmed people. People drank water with DDT. People ate foods with DDT. Too much DDT could kill a human.

DDT was long-lasting. It stayed in the ground. It stayed in animals. Think of a cow that eats grass sprayed with DDT. DDT gets in the cow's milk. A child drinks that milk. The DDT might harm the child, too.

One day, Carson got a note from a friend. "The plane flew over our small town," the note said. "The spray killed seven of our song birds."

Carson knew she had to act. She could tell people about DDT. She wrote a book called *Silent Spring.*

Silent Spring warned of the harm done by DDT. It told of an Earth with no birds left to sing. "The mistakes made now are being made for all time," Carson wrote.

Carson knew pests had to be stopped. But pesticides were bad. "Try other ways," she said. "Let nature work for us. Bring in ladybugs and spiders to kill harmful bugs."

Silent Spring caused a fight. "Stop the pesticides!" cried the news people. But not everyone liked Carson's book. Farmers had to keep their crops safe. Many people made money selling bug sprays. These people thought Carson was wrong. "We can live without birds," a man wrote, "but not without business."

Silent Spring had made its mark, though. Soon there were new laws. They controlled the use of pesticides. Rachel Carson's warnings were an important wake-up call. For now, the birds still sing.

3. What is DDT?

4. Why is DDT so harmful?

5. What is *Silent Spring* about?

6. Why did some people think Carson was wrong about DDT? Do you agree with them? Why? Why not?

7. Why do you think her book is called *Silent Spring*?

8. How can a book change history?

Laser Light

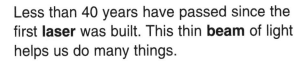

WORDS TO KNOW

laser (LAY-zuhr) a straight beam of light

beam (beem) a ray of light

Theodore Maiman (THEE-uh-dawr MAY-muhn) the man who made the first laser

source (sawrs) the thing or place from which something comes

bar codes (bahr cohdz) the black and white lines marked on store items

CDs (see-deez) disks that store sound, information, and other messages

Less than 40 years have passed since the first **laser** was built. This thin **beam** of light helps us do many things.

Think about a beam of light packed with power. Actors in the movies and TV shows fight with these beams of light. The beams are so powerful that they can stun or kill. Of course, these are just stories. But the idea is also very real. An American scientist, **Theodore Maiman**, made a new machine in 1960. It shot a mighty beam of light. This was the first laser.

A laser beam is not like normal light. Normal light is like light from the sun. It spreads out as it moves away from its **source**. Laser light doesn't spread out. It moves in a narrow line.

Laser light is special in a second way. It is made of just one color. Normal light is a mix of many colors. You can see this when sunlight passes through drops of water. You see a colorful rainbow.

The color of laser light depends on what is used in the machine. Early lasers used hard things. The first one used a ruby. It shot red light. Now lasers use liquids and gases, too.

1. When was the first laser made?

2. Name two ways laser light differs from normal light.

Today's laser gives off a very strong beam. It can punch a hole in steel. It can cut through a diamond. That's the hardest thing in the world. The laser can center its force on a tiny spot. It can drill 200 holes in the head of a pin.

Lasers are at work in factories. They cut and drill. The beam makes a clean cut or hole. Lasers can cut soft things as well as hard. Some are used to trim cloth. The beam seals the cut edges.

Lasers can take the place of the doctor's knife. The light cuts. Its heat seals the cut. There is little blood. Lasers can take spots off skin. The light burns away the spot. Yet the skin around it stays cool. Doctors use them to get rid of birthmarks or tattoos.

Eye doctors use lasers, too. The beam can pass into the eye. It can hit tiny spots that need fixing. Lasers help to improve eyesight.

Some dentists use lasers to drill teeth. The beam cuts away decay. It does not harm the tooth. It does not hurt the patient.

Lasers are at work in stores. They read the **bar codes** on boxes. They read the prices and the items.

Lasers are even at work in our homes. **CDs** are made with lasers. The letters "CD" stand for "**c**ompact **d**isk." The music signals are burned onto the disk. Inside a CD player, a laser reads the signals on the CD. Only light touches the CD. That's why CDs never get scratched.

There seems to be no end to the jobs lasers can do. They are at work in outer space. They are at work on phone lines. Their colored beams pulse with music at light shows. The age of the laser is here.

3. How do doctors use lasers?

4. Why don't CDs get scratched or worn out?

5. What makes lasers so special?

Math

Math is part of daily life. It helps you figure out how much exercise you need. It helps you find your way. It even helps you decide what to wear.

Exercise

WORDS TO KNOW

exercise (EHK-suhr-seyez) working your muscles to keep your body healthy

routine (roo-TEEN) the things you do regularly

Playing a sport or working out can be fun. But **exercise** is more than just fun. It helps your body. Learn how to make sure you get enough of the right kind of exercise.

We all want to be healthy. We want to feel good. We want to keep from getting sick. We want to have plenty of energy.

There is one way we can be healthier. We can exercise. When people exercise, they work their bodies by doing things like running. Exercise helps make the heart strong. It helps make muscles strong. The more you use your muscles, the stronger they get.

There are many ways you can exercise. You may already do some of these things. For example, you may walk a mile to school every day. You may ride your bike. You may play tennis or basketball.

All these are good ways to get exercise. To make exercise count, you should play or work out hard. Your breathing should get faster. You also have to exercise more than once in a while. You need to make exercise part of your weekly **routine**.

Doctors say you need to exercise for at least 30 minutes, 3 days a week. That adds up to 90 minutes of exercise a week.

1. How does exercise help your body?

2. How much exercise should you get each week?

You can find out if you are getting enough exercise. For a week, you can write down when you exercise. Write the date. Write what you do. Write how long you do it. Remember, you need to be working your body. Watching TV does not count as exercise!

Here's how one girl, Jill Lake, found out how much exercise she got in one week. She decided to write what exercise she did and how long she did it.

On Monday, she rode her bike. Before she set out, she looked at the time. Her watch said 3:35 P.M. Jill rode to her friend's house. The friend joined Jill. Together, they rode to the lake and back. Then Jill rode home. When she got home, she looked at her watch. It was 4:35 P.M. On a piece of paper, Jill wrote this: *Monday: bike riding, 60 minutes.*

On Tuesday and Wednesday, Jill got no exercise. On Thursday, she went to the swimming pool. She looked at the clock when she got in the pool. It said 5:10 P.M. Jill swam laps. She swam up and down the pool without stopping. When she got out, she looked at the clock again. It said 5:25 P.M. She took a break. Then she got back in the pool. She swam from 5:35 P.M. to 5:55 P.M.

She wrote this on her piece of paper: *Thursday: swimming, 15 minutes plus 20 minutes. Total: 35 minutes.*

On Friday, Jill went dancing. After she had been dancing for a few minutes, she remembered to look at the clock. It said 7:30 P.M. When she took a break, Jill looked at the clock again. It said 8:35 P.M. Jill saw she had been dancing for 65 minutes. She wrote this on her paper. *Friday: dancing, 65 minutes.*

Over the weekend, Jill was very busy. She did not exercise. On Sunday, she looked at her paper to find out how much exercise she had gotten during the week.

She had exercised on 3 days. Each day, she had exercised at least 30 minutes. Jill added her minutes of exercise. She had exercised 160 minutes. She had gotten more than the 90 minutes of exercise that doctors suggest. Jill was pleased. That was more than enough exercise for the week.

3. What three things did Jill do for exercise?

4. What was the difference in the amount of exercise Jill got on Thursday and Friday?

5. Did Jill get enough exercise for the week to stay healthy? Why? Why not?

6. How can you tell if you get enough exercise in a week?

7. What kinds of exercise could you do to stay healthy?

Changing Money

WORDS TO KNOW

Mexico (MEHK-sih-koh) a country south of the United States

pesos (PAY-sohz) the money used in Mexico

economy (ih-KAHN-uh-mee) the way things are bought and sold in a country

expensive (ihk-SPEHN-sihv) costing a lot of money

Each country uses a different type of money. In the United States, we use dollars. If you are going to another country, you may not be able to use dollars. You will need to get some of the money used in that country. Learn how one person did this.

Dan is excited. He is going to **Mexico** on vacation for a week. Dan knows he will not be able to use dollars there. In Mexico, they use **pesos** for money.

Dan thinks about how much money he will take to Mexico. He has already paid for his plane ticket and hotel. He figures he will need about $50 a day for food, sightseeing, and other things. For a 7-day trip, that comes to $350.

Before he leaves the United States, Dan goes to the bank. He writes a check on his bank account for $350. He wants to change the dollars into pesos.

At the bank, Dan learns that for $1, he will get 8 pesos. Dan wants to know how much 1 peso is worth in U.S. money. To do that, he divides 8 pesos into $1. He finds out that 1 peso is worth about 12 cents. "This will be easy," he thinks. "A peso is worth a little more than a dime. I can remember that."

Dan gives the bank the $350. The bank gives him 8 pesos for each dollar. That comes to 2,800 pesos.

1. How did Dan figure how much money to take to Mexico?

2. How many pesos did Dan get for $1?

Dan arrives in Mexico. Soon, he gets used to using pesos. If he sees a sign for something that costs 8 pesos, he knows that it costs about one U.S. dollar. If he sees a sign for something that costs 16 pesos, he knows it costs about $2.

Dan is surprised to find that meals cost much less than he thought they would. He can get a very large breakfast of eggs, bean tacos, orange juice, and milk for about 4 pesos. That's only $.50 for a lot of food.

One day Dan talks to the man who serves him breakfast. "Breakfast here is much cheaper than in the United States," Dan tells the man.

"Yes," the man says, "the peso is not worth what it once was."

"What do you mean?" Dan asks.

"Just last year, the peso was worth more," the man explained. "If you had been here last year, you would have gotten 5 pesos for a dollar, not 8."

Dan thinks about this. He does some quick math. If he could get 5 pesos for $1, a peso would be worth 20 cents. A 4-peso breakfast would cost $.80, not $.50.

"Why is that?" Dan asks the man.

"Our **economy** is having some trouble. When that happens, our money is worth less. It buys less. Your economy is doing better. Your money is strong. It is worth more. So it is very good for you when you come to visit. You get many pesos for a dollar. But it is very **expensive** for us to go to your country. It costs us a lot."

The man explains, " I went to the United States last year. I got $1 for 5 pesos. If something cost $10, I needed 50 pesos. If I went to the United States today, it would take 8 pesos to buy $1. If something costs $10, I would need 80 pesos, not 50. See?"

Dan nods. He hopes the Mexican economy gets better. But he is glad the money in the

United States is strong. This trip is costing less than he planned. But Dan also knows that this could change. Next year, the same trip could cost more.

3. If Dan's trip had taken place last year, would it have cost him more or less? Why?

4. When an economy gets stronger, what happens to its money? Why?

5. You are taking a trip to a country that had a strong economy last year. This year, that same country has a weak economy. Will the trip be more expensive or less expensive this year? Why?

6. What's the best way to figure out how many dollars or parts of dollars are in a country's type of money?

Weather Temperatures

People like to know how hot or cold it is. They also like to know if it's hotter or colder than usual. Learn how the weather people figure this out.

You may watch TV news. If you do, you will hear about the weather. You may hear the high **temperature** for the day. That is the hottest it was that day. The weather person may call it the "high" of the day.

You may hear the low temperature for the day. That is the coldest it got that day. The weather person on television may call this the "low" of the day.

Then, you may hear the **average** high for that date. That is the middle of all the highs for that date over a certain number of years.

You may also hear the average low. That is the middle of all the lows for that date over a certain number of years.

People like to know these things. They like to know the average high and low. They like to know if it is warmer or colder than average. You may have heard a friend say it is really warm this year. Maybe she remembers it was hot on this day last year. Maybe she knows the average highs and lows. She knows it is warmer than average.

1. What is the high temperature of a day?
   What is the low?

2. What is an average high for a date?
   What is an average low?

About 100 years ago, people started writing down what the weather was each day. In a few years, they had many weather facts. They could use these facts to figure out many things. One thing they could figure is the average high.

Here's how they figure it out. Let's say you live in Dallas, a city in **Texas**. You want to know the average high for July 15. You go to the library. There you look up all the highs for that date. One year, the high was 101 **degrees,** or 101°. Another year, it was 80°. A third year, the high was 89°. You may find highs for 75 years. You write all these numbers down.

When you're done, you have 75 highs for July 15. There is one high for each year. Add these numbers. You may get a huge number. For July 15, it is 6,600°.

To find out the average high, divide 6,600°

by the number of years. The number of years is 75. Dividing 6,600 by 75, you get 88°. That is the average high for July 15 in Dallas.

You can also find the average low for that date. You write the lows for that date for the past 75 years. Then you add those numbers. In Dallas for July 15, you get 6,375°. You divide that number by 75 years. The average low in Dallas for July 15 is 85°. Dallas is a pretty hot place in July as you can see on the TV screen below.

Today's High: 93⁰
Today's Low : 89⁰
Average High: 88⁰
Average Low: 85⁰

AB WEATHER REPORT

The highs and lows for other places are different. The average highs and lows for July 15 in Nome, a city in **Alaska**, are much lower. Nome is much cooler than Dallas.

Knowing all this can be helpful. You may go on a trip. You may go to a place you do not know. You can look in a book about the place. The book will tell you more about the weather there. It will list the average highs and lows. You will know what to pack. If you know it is usually hot, you won't bring your winter coat!

3. How do you find the average high for a date?

4. How do you find the average low for a date?

5. Why are the average highs and lows for different places different?

6. Why would a person want to know the average highs and lows?

7. Why are people so interested in the weather?

Road Maps

WORDS TO KNOW

distance (DIHS-tuhns) the amount of space between two things or places

road map (rohd map) a kind of map that shows highways and streets

scale (skayl) a distance on a map that stands for a longer distance

represents (rehp-rih-ZEHNTZ) stands for something

routes (rootz; rowtz) ways to travel someplace

If you have a map, you can figure out the **distance** between two places. If there's more than one way to get from one place to another, you can find which way is shorter.

Maps can be very useful. If you are planning a car trip, you can use a **road map**. The map will show you which roads to take. It will show how far you'll have to go.

Look at the map of Lile County. At the bottom on the right, you see a line. It says "**scale**." The scale tells how many miles a distance on the map is in the real world. On this map, 1 inch **represents** 10 miles in the real world. You can also say 1 inch equals 10 miles on this map.

Here's how to use the scale. Find the sports fields on the map. Now find Lile City. To find how far apart they are, measure the space between them. There is 1 inch between them on the map.

To find out how many miles 1 inch represents, look at the scale. It tells you that 1 inch equals 10 miles. There is 1 inch between the sports fields and Lile City. So it must be 10 miles from the sports fields to Lile City.

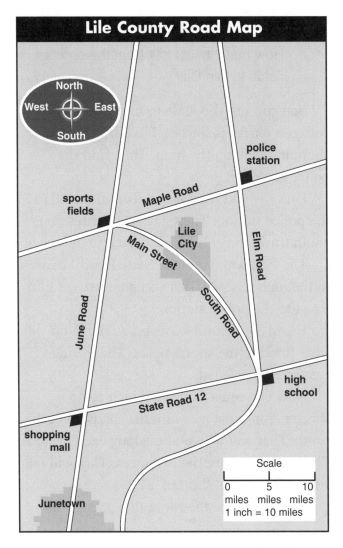

Lile County Road Map

North
West — East
South

police
station

sports
fields

Maple Road

Lile
City

Elm Road

Main Street

South Road

June Road

high
school

State Road 12

shopping
mall

Scale

0   5   10
miles   miles   miles
1 inch = 10 miles

Junetown

1. What is the scale on a map?

2. How many miles is it from the sports fields to Lile City?

You can use the scale to find which way between places is shorter. First, find the shopping mall on the map. Then find the police station.

Let's say you need to get from the mall to the police station. There are two **routes** you could travel to get from one place to the other.

The first way, you take State Road 12 east to the high school. Then you go north on Elm Road to the police station.

Using the second way, you go north on June Road to the sports fields. Then you go east on Maple Road.

Now you must find out which route is shorter. You must measure the roads on each route. That will tell you how long each route is. Then you compare the distances. That will tell you which way is shorter.

First, measure the route that goes by the

high school. Using a ruler, find the distance between the mall and the high school. It is 2 inches. You know 1 inch represents 10 miles. To find the distance between the mall and the high school, you multiply 2 inches by 10 miles. It is 20 miles from the shopping mall to the high school.

Now measure from the high school to the police station on Elm Road. It is also 2 inches. You know this part of the route is 20 miles on State Road 12 plus 20 miles on Elm Road. The trip is 40 miles using this route.

Now measure the route that goes by the sports fields. Measure the distance from the mall to the sports fields on June Road. It is 2 inches. Since 1 inch represents 10 miles, multiply 2 inches by 10. It is 20 miles from the mall to the sports fields.

Next, measure the distance from the sports fields to the police station. It is $1\frac{1}{2}$ inches. To find out how far this is, you multiply 1 inch by 10 and get 10 miles. Then you figure how many miles are represented by $\frac{1}{2}$ inch. To do this, multiply 10 by $\frac{1}{2}$. It is 5 miles. So it is 15 miles altogether from the sports fields to the police station on Maple Road.

To find the length of the whole second route, add 20 miles to 15 miles. It is 35 miles.

To find which route is shorter, look at the two distances. One route, from the mall to the high school and then to the police station, is 40 miles. The other route, from the mall to the sports fields and then to the police station, is 35 miles. The route of 35 miles is shorter because 35 is smaller than 40.

3. How can you tell the number of miles from one place to another on this map?

4. Compare the distance from the shopping mall to the police station using the two routes. Which way would you go? Why?

5. Do you think scales on all maps are the same? Why or why not?

6. In what ways can a map and its scale help you?

Life Skills

Being prepared is wise. These readings will tell you what to do during accidents or disasters. They will help you move or even buy a used car.

Buying a Used Car

WORDS TO KNOW

exhaust (ihg-ZAWST) smoke and used gases

tune-up (TOON-up) changes that make an engine run better

idle (EYED-uhl) run slowly while out of gear

transmission (tranz-MIHSH-uhn) a car part that sends power from the engine to the wheels

mechanic (mih-KAN-ihk) a worker who knows about and fixes cars

bargain (BAHR-gihn) to talk with a seller to try to get the price lowered

---

There are millions of used cars for sale. A lot of them are junk. But some are great buys. Here are a few hints to help you buy a great used car.

"Here's how it is, Mom," says Matt. "If I had my own car, I wouldn't use yours. I could run errands for you. You know I'm a careful driver. I'm always home on time. And hey, you had a car when you were 16."

And so another teenager plots and plans and argues. "It just makes good sense," Matt points out. "I should have a car!"

Let's say Matt's parents give in. They agree he should buy a car. Like most teens, Matt has little money. The car he buys will probably be used. Used cars cost much less than new cars.

Someone else wants Matt to buy a car, too. Someone wants him to have a car even more than he wants one. It's the person selling the used car. He or she hopes Matt will buy a car and buy it soon!

But Matt is too smart for that. He is going to take his time.

First, he does some reading. Matt looks at books about buying a used car. They explain what to look for. They list questions to ask. They tell how much money some used cars are worth. They tell how safe each car is.

They tell how often each car needs to be fixed.

Now Matt is ready to look for a car. He goes to used car dealers. He checks newspaper ads for cars sold by their owners. He finds a car that sounds right for him.

1. Why do most teens buy used cars?

2. What does Matt do before he looks for a used car?

But Matt is not ready to buy a car just yet. He must do something important first. He must take the car for a test drive. He must check it for problems.

To start the test drive, Matt turns on the engine. The first thing he checks is the steering. With the car in park, Matt sticks his head out the window. He watches the front tire as he turns the steering wheel. The tire should start to move as soon as he starts to turn the wheel. If the steering wheel turns more than 2 inches before the tires move, there could be problems.

Now Matt is ready to drive. He takes the car on a highway. He takes some side streets around town. He finds a bumpy road so he can check for rattles and squeaks.

As he drives, Matt checks the **exhaust**. He looks in the rear-view mirror. He watches the smoke that comes out of the tail pipe. Blue smoke can mean engine problems. Black smoke means the car may just need a **tune-up**. White smoke can be water that built up while the car was off. The white smoke should stop after he drives for a while. If it doesn't, that's bad. Water from the radiator may be leaking into the engine.

Matt stops. He checks the brakes. He makes sure the car does not pull to the side when he stops. If it does, the brakes may need to be fixed. Matt pushes the brake pedal down as far as he can. It should go no closer than $1\frac{1}{2}$ inches to the floor. He keeps the pedal down for a minute. If it sinks lower during that time, there could be big brake problems.

Now Matt checks to see that the wheels are in line. He finds a straight, flat road. When it's safe, he lets go of the steering wheel for a second. The car should not pull to one side. It should move in a straight line.

Matt wants a great radio in his car, but he turns it off for now. He needs to hear the engine. Out on the road, he listens for strange sounds. Even though it is cold, Matt rolls down the window. He wants to hear every car noise. He listens for a ping or tap from the engine.

Matt pulls over again. He lets the engine **idle**. It should sound smooth. Again, Matt listens for odd sounds. He should not hear any loud tapping.

Now Matt listens to the **transmission**. He puts his foot on the brake. He shifts from park to drive to reverse. He should hear soft thumps or no noise at all. He doesn't want to hear clanks. Clanks mean trouble!

Matt checks the heater. He checks the air conditioner. He tries all settings. He puts his hands over the vents. He checks to see if the air blowing out is cold. Once again, Matt listens for odd sounds.

Now Matt turns off the engine. The car should stop right away.

After the test drive, Matt checks the body of the car. He looks for rust. He looks for water leaks. The body is almost as important as the engine. He won't buy the car if the body is not in good shape.

When he's done, Matt talks to the owner. He asks questions. He wants to know what's been fixed in the past. He wants to know if the car has been in any accidents.

Matt loves this car. But he's still not ready to buy. Matt takes the car to his parents' **mechanic**. He reports the sounds he heard during the test drive. He tells the mechanic about the car's past. The mechanic checks the car. This costs Matt $40. But those dollars spent now can save Matt a lot later.

Matt asks the mechanic what needs to be fixed. He asks how much these repairs will cost. He can use this information to **bargain** for a lower price on the car.

The mechanic tells Matt the car is in pretty good shape. Finally, Matt is ready to buy his first car!

3. What is the first thing Matt checks during the test drive?

4. Why do you think brakes should be one of the first things to check?

5. Tell how Matt checks the transmission.

6. How can a test drive help you to choose the right car?

7. Why is it smart to have a used car checked by a mechanic?

8. If a seller does not want you to test drive the car or take it to a mechanic, what should you do? Why?

Moving

WORDS TO KNOW

reserve (rih-ZERV) set aside for later use

forward (FAWR-wuhrd) send on to a new address

transfer (TRANS-fuhr) change from one place to another

Sometimes a new job may take people to a new place. At other times people just want a larger house or apartment. Most Americans move many times. Moving is a lot of work, though. Here are some tips to make it easier.

Moving to a new home can be an adventure. But it can also be a big job. To make the job easier, start early. Break it into small tasks. Here's how.

It is one month before moving day! This is the time to make some calls. You may need to rent a truck if you are moving your own things. Call now to **reserve** one. That way, you know that a truck will have been set aside for you when you need it. If you are hiring a moving company, call and set up the dates.

Get the things you'll need for packing. You will need boxes, newspaper, tape, and rope. If you are using a moving company, check with them. They have a lot of the things you'll need.

You can start packing. For now, just pack things you won't need in the next month. Don't pack important things and papers. Put them where you can get to them.

With just one month until the move, it's time to go to the post office. Fill out a change–of–address card. The post office will **forward** mail to your new address.

The post office also has cards that you can send out. Use them to tell people and businesses about your move. Send one to your bank. Send one to insurance and credit card companies. Don't forget doctors and dentists. Send the cards to your friends, too. That way they will have your new address. It will be nice to hear from them in your new home.

1. Name one thing you can do a month before you move.

2. Where would you send change-of-address cards? Name two places.

There are two weeks until moving day! It's time to pick up the phone again. Call the gas, electric, and water companies. Call the oil company. Call the cable TV and phone companies. Let them know when to stop service at your old address. Sign up for service at your new one.

If you plan to move yourself, stop and think. You'll need help lifting and carrying things on moving day. It's time to call on friends and family. Ask them to help.

Keep on packing. As you pack, label each box. List what is inside. Tell which room the things go in. Number the boxes. Keep a separate list of what is in each box. Mark all boxes that hold things that can break.

Think of what you might need during the move. Don't put those things in a box. Pack a bag with pills, maps, food, drinks, and a change of clothes. Keep it in a place that is easy to find.

It's just 24 hours to moving day! Collect the things you'll need. A pocket knife is useful. Pens, a tape measure, and scissors will come in handy, too. Pads or sheets will keep furniture safe from scratches. Pick up the truck if you have rented one.

You should be all set for the big day. Load the truck and go.

You may think you are done. But moving out is just half the job. The other half is moving in.

It's one week after moving day. You did it! Most of the boxes are unpacked. Now, take a look at your new neighborhood. Check the nearby stores. Look for things you'll need. Look for a new bank, dry cleaners, and supermarket. Find the hospital. Find the police and fire stations.

Students, be sure to sign up at your new school. Voters, sign up to vote. Drivers, if you are in a new state, **transfer** your license. You'll need a license from your new state.

You can call town offices to ask about trash pickup, parks, and libraries. Be sure to talk to your new neighbors. They often have the best hints of all.

3. Why should you label each box you pack?

4. What are the three places in a new neighborhood you might need in an emergency?

5. Where can you get information about your new neighborhood?

6. What do you think might happen if you didn't plan your move well ahead of time?

First Aid

Even when people are careful, accidents do happen. You may be there when an accident occurs. You may be called on to help.

"I've cut myself!" José cried. Darla ran to see. His hand was bleeding. It looked bad. "Help me," José said weakly. José was lucky. Darla knew just what to do.

We all need to know first aid. First aid is quick care for a person who has been hurt or has become ill. Remember, the goal of first aid is to save lives and stop further harm. It never takes the place of a doctor's care.

The following tips deal with cuts and burns. But there's much more to know. Your home should have a good first aid book. Keep it where you can find it. Read it over. You should learn first aid now. Once an accident happens, it may be too late.

A person who has been badly cut or burned may go into **shock**. Shock is dangerous. The body slows down. Always check for the signs of shock. These signs can happen with almost any injury. The skin may be pale, cold, and damp. It may be spotty. Breathing may be weak or uneven.

If you think a person is in shock, act fast.

Lay the **victim** down. (If the back or neck is hurt, do not move the victim.) If the person has trouble breathing, raise the neck and shoulders. Otherwise, raise the legs and feet so they are higher than the head. Keep the victim warm. Call for a doctor's help.

1. Why should you keep a first aid book where you can find it?

2. What are the signs of shock?

Cuts often need first aid. Skin is most often cut on knives, metal, broken glass, or other sharp things. Bleeding may be heavy. Seek a doctor's help for heavy bleeding. Use first aid until help gets there.

Stop the bleeding. First, try pressing on the cut. Use a clean cloth or a bandage. Try not to get blood on you. In most cases, the bleeding will stop. Do not remove the cloth. If one piece soaks through, add more layers. Keep pressing. Raise the cut part of the body. Make sure it's higher than the heart.

When the bleeding stops, bandage the cut firmly but not too tightly. Check the **pulse** below the wound. If you can't feel it beating, loosen the bandage until it returns.

Sometimes, pressing the cut does not stop the bleeding. There are certain other spots on the body you can press. You can press these spots to control the flow of blood. If a hand is cut, place your thumb on the inner side of the victim's wrist. Press toward the bone. The bleeding should stop. A first aid book will tell you where to find other places to press.

Burns are also common. They may be caused by a match, a stove, hot water, or the sun's rays. Most burns come from heat.

Before treating a heat burn, decide how bad it is. Red skin means a **first-degree burn**. This is the least serious burn. Blisters and red or spotted skin mean a **second-degree burn**. White skin means a **third-degree burn**. Third-degree burns are very serious.

Apply cold water to a first-degree burn. This will help the pain. Cover with a dry bandage. This will keep the burn clean.

Soak a second-degree burn in cold water until the pain stops. Do not use ice water to soak. Then apply clean cloths that have been wrung out in ice water. Take the cloths off. Gently pat the skin dry. Cover loosely with a dry, clean bandage. A person with second-degree burns should see a doctor as soon as possible.

If you think that a victim has third-degree burns, call for a doctor's help right away. Do not put water, sprays, or creams on the burns. Do not remove clothes from the burns.

Cover the third-degree burns lightly with a dry, clean sheet or cloth. Raise the burned area higher than the heart. Treat for shock. Then wait for the doctor. People with third-degree burns need to be in a hospital.

There are certain things you shouldn't do with any kind of burn. Never break blisters. Do not remove burned skin. Do not use sprays or creams. Avoid pressing on the burned areas. All of these things can make burns worse.

These are just a few first aid tips. There's a

lot more to know. You can learn how to help others who are hurt. You can learn how to help yourself. The Red Cross gives classes in first aid. They put out books to use as guides. Whether you are a son or a daughter, a baby-sitter, a parent, a neighbor, or a friend, you need to know first aid.

3. What is the aim of first aid for cuts?

4. Why should you decide what kind of burn the victim has before you give first aid?

5. How are first-, second-, and third-degree burns the same? How are they different?

6. Why do you think it would be important for a baby-sitter to know first aid?

Disasters

Wind storms. Floods. Earthquakes. We don't
think of these things until it's too late. You can't
stop disasters from happening. But you can be
ready for them. Know what to do. It could save
your life or someone else's.

People put up homes near the sea. Then big storms blow in from the water. People build towns along rivers. Then rivers flood. People pave roads over **fault lines**. Then the earth cracks and shakes. To live almost anywhere, people must be ready when nature goes to extremes.

Different places have different **natural** disasters. In some places, rivers flood. In others, big winds blow. In still other places, the earth may shake. But there are ways to stay safe. Here are some basic rules.

Find out which natural disasters may strike your area. Read about ways to prepare. Go over these plans with your family.

Be prepared by getting your home ready. Stock ready-to-eat food and bottled water. Put together or buy a first aid kit. Buy candles and flashlights. Have a radio that runs on batteries. Choose a good place to keep all of these things together. You might not have time to look for them later.

During a disaster, you should listen to the radio or to TV. Local stations will let you know what's going on.

1. List three natural disasters that may happen.

2. Name one thing you should have in your home in case of any disaster.

Some storms can blow the roof off a house. A **hurricane** is a big wind storm. It moves in from the sea. You have time to prepare before a hurricane strikes.The most important thing to remember is to act as soon as you have warning.

Protect your home against the storm. Close shutters and board up windows. Tie down outdoor things. Tie boats to docks or take them out of the water. Fill bathtubs, bottles, and jars with water.

Get out of any place that is not strong. Leave a mobile home or trailer. Turn off electric power, gas, and water before you leave. Find a strong building to stay in.

Stay indoors during a hurricane. Keep away from windows. The safest place is a small room with strong walls or a basement. Get under a big table if there is no other safe place.

A **tornado** is another kind of storm with strong winds. It is a fast, swirling wind. It can come with thunder and lightning. If a tornado is coming, you must get to safety right away. You may have only a few minutes before it strikes. Go to a storm cellar or basement. You can also stay in a room in the middle of the house.

If you are outside during a tornado, lie in a ditch. Cover your head. Pull clothing over your face to keep out dust.

Some storms bring lightning. A lightning bolt can kill. These rules may keep you safe when lightning strikes.

Stay in a building or a car. During the storm, don't use electric power or the phone. Don't touch metal. Stay away from windows, doors, and fireplaces. Don't try to cook or take a bath when there is lightning.

If you are outside, stay away from high places. Keep away from wire fences, metal poles, and tall trees. Get in a cave or ditch. Crawl under low bushes. Do not go in the water. Stay off small boats.

Be very careful if your hair stands up and your skin tingles. That means lightning is near. Drop to the ground and lie flat.

When the hurricane, tornado, or lightning storm ends, stay away from electricity for a while. Wait to use the phone. Be careful not to touch downed power lines.

The storm may be over, but disaster may still strike. If the rain has been heavy, there may be a flood. Learn the rules of flood safety.

Floods can poison drinking water. When flood warnings go up, store water. Fill bathtubs, bottles, and jars. After a flood, boil tap water before drinking it. Be careful not to eat or drink anything that flood water has touched. Wash well to remove germs if you've been in flood waters.

A flood may force you from your home.

If you must leave, turn off electric power. Turn off the gas and the water, too.

Never drive a car through flood water. It is dangerous to walk in water over your knees. When you walk or drive, watch out for road slides. Do not go near fallen wires.

In most cases, you will know when a flood or a storm is on the way. But an earthquake strikes without warning. Be ready before the earth shakes. Here are a few ways to prepare.

Store enough food and water for a few days. Then check your home for earthquake dangers. Bolt down water heaters. Make sure gas lines are tight. Broken gas lines can cause fires.

When the ground shakes, most harm comes from falling things. Keep heavy things on low shelves. Fasten shelves to walls. Stay away from high shelves, windows, and mirrors. Find a safe spot inside. Get under a table, desk, or bed. Stand in a strong doorway.

If you are outside, stay away from tall buildings or power poles. They could fall.

Move to an open place. If you're in a car, try to stop out in the open.

When the shaking gets weaker, don't think it's over. Expect more shaking. There may be **aftershocks**. These won't be as strong as the first quake. Still, they can cause some damage.

We can't stop these acts of nature. Winds will blow. Rivers will flood. The earth will shake. But people can be ready. We can learn how to deal with disasters.

3. What can you do to get ready for a hurricane?

4. Why must you get to safety right away if a tornado is coming?

5. Why might there be danger even after a storm is over?

6. What causes the most harm during an earthquake?

7. What can you do to prepare for disasters in your area?